THE DEADLY DOLL

BY J. BURKE
ILLUSTRATED BY SHAUN TAN
COVER ILLUSTRATION BY CHIP BOLES

Librarian Reviewer
Marci Peschke
Librarian, Dallas Independent School District
MA Education Reading Specialist, Stephen F. Austin State University
Learning Resources Endorsement, Texas Women's University

Reading Consultant
Elizabeth Stedem
Educator/Consultant, Colorado Springs, CO
MA in Elementary Education, University of Denver, CO

STONE ARCH BOOKS
Minneapolis   San Diego

First published in the United States in 2008
by Stone Arch Books
151 Good Counsel Drive, P.O. Box 669
Mankato, Minnesota 56002
www.stonearchbooks.com

First published in Australia in 1997 by Lothian Books
(now Hachette Livre Australia Pty Ltd)

Published in arrangement with Hachette Livre Australia.

Library of Congress Cataloging-in-Publication Data
Burke, Janine, 1952–
    [Doll]
    The Deadly Doll / by J. Burke; illustrated by Shaun Tan.
    p. cm. — (Shade Books)
    Summary: When Claudine's family receives in the mail
a beautiful old French doll that has been in the family for
generations, no one anticipates its malevolent intentions.
    ISBN-13: 978-1-59889-858-3 (library binding)
    ISBN-10: 1-59889-858-2 (library binding)
    ISBN-13: 978-1-59889-914-6 (paperback)
    ISBN-10: 1-59889-914-7 (paperback)
    [1. Dolls—Fiction. 2. Horror stories.] I. Tan, Shaun, ill.
II. Title.
PZ7.B9193De 2008
[Fic]—dc22   2007003720

Art Director: Heather Kindseth
Graphic Designer: Kay Fraser

1 2 3 4 5 6 12 11 10 09 08 07

Printed in the United States of America

Table of Contents

CHAPTER 1

LITTLE LIZZIE

"Caroline! Come quickly."

The girl got up from her seat in the garden and tossed down the book she had been reading. She yawned and stretched. What did Mom want now?

Caroline thought about her list of chores. Her mother loved lists.

Since Caroline's new sister, Annie, had been born, Mom had been busier than ever. She got a real kick out of having everything in the house running perfectly, and her energy was amazing.

She was up first thing in the morning and zoomed through the day.

Caroline was the dreamy type. She always had her head stuck in a book. Sometimes she felt like she and her mother were from different planets.

Opening the doors from the garden, Caroline stepped into the living room.

The house was quiet. Annie was asleep.

Mom was on her knees on the floor, surrounded by pieces of wrapping paper. Next to her was a huge cardboard box.

"Look what we've been sent from France!" Mom held up a large doll.

It was the biggest doll Caroline had ever seen.

It was nearly three feet high. Blond hair fell in shiny curls to the doll's shoulders. Its big, blue, glass eyes stared at the world.

The doll's china skin was pale pink and its lips curved in a perfect red smile.

Its flowered dress had a lace collar and cuffs. Its shoes were shiny black leather and had little gold buckles. Even the socks were lace.

"Isn't she beautiful?" cried Mom. "Look! Her name is Little Lizzie. Well, that's what it says on her tag. She's from France."

She put the doll on the floor. It stared at Caroline.

Mom continued, "She's from your grandma's house. Your aunt sent her. I know you never met Granny Montand, but she always sent you presents. She was interested in everything you did." Mom looked sad. "Her death last year was horrible for your father."

Caroline remembered the phone call that had come late one night.

Her dad had talked very fast in French to his sister. After he'd put down the phone, Dad had stood silently with his head in his hands.

Caroline nodded. "Yes, I used to like getting Granny's letters."

Mom and Dad would often talk about how great it would be to visit the family in France, but somehow they had never gotten around to it.

Mom patted the doll's hair. "You'll take care of her, won't you? After all, your sister is just a baby. She's too young for dolls."

Caroline wrinkled her nose in disgust. "No thanks. She's all yours, Mom."

Caroline's mom looked at her. "What on earth do you mean?" she said.

Caroline said, "I'm almost thirteen, you know. I don't really like dolls anymore."

Ever since she was little, Caroline had collected old dolls. She had eight, and all of them were kept on a special shelf in her bedroom.

She still liked them, but she had other interests now.

The dolls were part of her childhood. They were kid stuff.

Caroline's mom sighed. "I just can't understand you, Caroline. I would have given anything for a doll like this when I was your age. I would have loved her," Mom said, staring into the doll's eyes.

Caroline sighed. That was just like Mom. She made a big deal out of everything.

"Okay, fine," Caroline said. "Give her to me and I'll be the babysitter until Annie's ready for her." She grabbed the doll.

"Careful!" cried Mom. "This doll is special. She's been in the family for over a hundred years."

"Just another reason to put her safely away," said Caroline.

She tucked the doll under her arm and headed for the stairs.

Little Lizzie refused to sit on the low wooden shelf with the other dolls.

Every time Caroline tried to put it gently on the shelf, all the other dolls ended up falling to the floor.

"Okay," she said, "I guess you'd better have your own private seat if you can't get along with everybody else."

She put Little Lizzie on the white wicker chair in the corner of her room. Then she put away a pile of clean clothes.

She kept glancing at the doll out of the corner of her eye.

It was hard not to look at Little Lizzie. Her big, blue glass eyes seemed to follow Caroline around the room.

There was something creepy about those eyes, something cold. It was as if, when Caroline stared at them, time and space started to disappear, and an icy blue pit opened up.

"Lunch!" Mom called, and Caroline jumped.

How long had she been staring at Little Lizzie? Why did she have the feeling that in those cold blue eyes there was a powerful force, a force as strong as life itself?

CHAPTER 2

BURNING UP

After lunch, Mom said she felt tired. That was weird. She was usually up and doing things for the whole day.

When Mom told Caroline she might go upstairs and take a nap, Caroline didn't mind. She would take care of Annie. Caroline loved looking after her little sister.

Caroline looked at her mother carefully. "You do look kind of pale, Mom," she said. "I hope you're not getting a cold or something."

Mom smiled. "Just tired. That's all. I just need a good, long nap. How about we make a chocolate cake later on?"

Even though she sounded okay, Mom's face was pale. She looked as if she had been up all night.

Caroline felt sorry for her mother. She worked really hard around the house. Maybe it was getting her down. Caroline knew she should help more.

"Take it easy, Mom. And don't worry, I'll take care of Annie," she said.

She watched as her mother walked up the stairs like a sleepwalker.

Caroline picked up Annie and cuddled her.

Annie was such a cute little girl.

She cooed and gurgled. Caroline made crazy faces and silly noises to get her sister to laugh.

Having a baby sister was definitely fun.

Suddenly, Caroline heard a thud and then a low groan coming from upstairs. She put Annie safely in her stroller. Then she raced up the stairs two at a time.

Her mom had fallen out of bed. When Caroline reached her, her skin was hot and damp. She helped her mom back into bed and brought her a glass of water.

Caroline's mom sipped the water slowly. "Sorry, honey," she mumbled. "I don't know what's wrong with me. I feel sort of dizzy, that's all."

"Okay, Mom. Just relax." Caroline decided that as soon as her dad got home, they would call the doctor.

She touched her mom's forehead. It was burning up.

Then Caroline saw Little Lizzie. It was sitting on the big armchair that faced the bed, staring at Mom with those huge, cold blue eyes.

How on earth had the doll moved from Caroline's bedroom? Mom must have brought it in. But when? And why?

Mom's eyelids fluttered and she whispered a few words that Caroline could not understand.

Caroline looked at Little Lizzie. It seemed like the doll was enjoying every moment of Mom's sickness.

The doll's little mouth seemed to have turned up slightly at the edges. It looked as if the doll was smiling even more.

Caroline looked carefully at Little Lizzie's perfect face.

No, it must have been a trick of the light. Of course Little Lizzie wasn't smiling. How silly!

Yet for a moment, just for a moment, it seemed as if the doll was grinning. It seemed like it saw, and liked, Mom's illness.

Anyway, Little Lizzie was giving Caroline the creeps. "Maybe you'd like to go to the spare room," she said, "with all the other junk."

Caroline picked up the doll and carried it to the spare room at the end of the hall.

The spare room was where Caroline's family kept things. Old tennis rackets, clothes, shoes, folding chairs, tents, and photo albums were piled on top of one another. There was even an ax in a corner of the room.

Mom often said that she would go into the spare room and clean it out from top to bottom. But then one of the family members would bring in another load of junk. The mess never ended.

"Welcome to your new home, kiddo," announced Caroline.

She found the large box that Little Lizzie had arrived in. It was stuffed with wrapping paper.

Caroline shoved the doll in, head first.

As she did, a small white envelope that had been taped inside the box came loose.

When she looked closely at it, Caroline saw that it had no name or address.

All that was written on it were the words "The History of Little Lizzie."

She was just about to open it when she heard the sound of her father's car.

Pushing the envelope into the pocket of her sweater, Caroline hurried downstairs.

CHAPTER 3

A STRANGE STORY

"**Q**uite frankly, I'm worried," said Dr. Simons as he stood with Caroline's dad at the front door. "Your wife has a very high fever. She might be coming down with that flu that's going around. I hope it's nothing more serious. Call me in the morning if there's no change."

"What happens then?" Caroline's father asked nervously.

Dr. Simons sighed. "We might need to put her into the hospital."

Listening in the living room, Caroline felt cold. The hospital. That was for people who were really sick.

Annie had started crying as soon as the doctor arrived, and hadn't stopped. It was like the baby knew that something bad was happening to her mother. She knew it and she was scared.

Caroline had been rocking the baby, but it wasn't helping.

Annie wanted her mother and wanted her now. Her little face was red and her screams tore through the house.

When Dad came into the living room, his face was serious. He tried to smile, which somehow made everything worse.

Caroline felt a knot tighten around her heart.

"How are my two favorite girls?" Dad said gently.

"Mom's going to be all right, isn't she?" Caroline asked quietly.

Dad gently stroked Caroline's hair. "Yes, of course." But he didn't sound like he believed it.

After tomato soup and grilled cheese sandwiches for dinner, Dad and Caroline sat in the dining room.

Mom hadn't been able to eat the soup Dad had made. She had tried, but she just didn't seem to have the energy, even though she was being fed.

All she asked for was more water. Then she drifted off to sleep.

Caroline rocked Annie. They had given her a bottle and, after a while, she had settled down, just crying now and then.

"Guess what, Dad? We got a present from France," said Caroline, trying to take her dad's mind off of her mom.

"Did we?" said her father. His mind seemed far away.

"Yeah, a great big doll. It came from Granny in France, and Mom thinks it's been in the family for a hundred years," Caroline said.

That got her father's attention. He scratched his head. "Oh, yes. That doll. Little Lizzie. There's a story about it. A strange story, actually, kind of a mystery."

Then Mom called out. Caroline and her father jumped to their feet and rushed upstairs.

Mom was sitting up in bed, smiling.

She still looked pale, but her fever had gone down.

Next to her on the bed was Little Lizzie. Its blue eyes were looking at Caroline's mom, and its mean little fingers were pointing toward her.

"Mom, where did you get that?" Caroline asked.

"Isn't she beautiful?" Mom said, patting the doll's blond hair.

"Mom, please listen to me," Caroline said. "Where did you find Little Lizzie?"

"What do you mean? She was sitting on the bed when I woke up." Mom laughed. "I think she's keeping me company."

"She's making you feel better," Caroline's father said. He looked happy.

Caroline looked from her mother to her father. "But, Mom, I put that doll away," she said, feeling very confused.

"Not now, Caroline," Dad said sternly. "Don't bother your mother. Perhaps you'd like some of that soup now, honey? You've got to build your strength up."

When Mom nodded, Caroline was sent downstairs to heat up the soup.

She thought to herself, I put that doll in the spare room. A doll can't get out of a box and walk down the hall.

Can it?

CHAPTER 4

ANOTHER ANNIE

That night, Caroline couldn't sleep. It was great that Mom was getting better, but there was something weird going on.

What had her dad said? There was some strange story about the doll. A mystery. Caroline sat up in bed and tried to figure it out.

Okay, she said to herself. Let's try to be calm about this.

She thought about the day's events in her mind.

She had taken Little Lizzie from the chair in Mom's room. Then she had put the doll in the spare room.

The doll had been stuffed in a box. Half an hour later it was sitting on Mom's bed.

Mom had been feeling really weird. Maybe she had wandered down the hall, opened the door to the spare room, and taken the doll out.

Mom had been so excited about Little Lizzie when it arrived. She thought it was the best thing since sliced bread. Maybe since she was sick, she didn't remember doing it.

It was possible.

Was it also possible that Little Lizzie had been able to get out of the box, walk down the hall, and climb onto her mom's bed?

Was it possible that the doll had done that not only once but twice?

After all, Caroline had left the doll sitting on the chair in her room before lunch.

Caroline shivered. Those cold blue eyes, those mean little fingers, that creepy smile when Little Lizzie was watching her mom. It was as if she enjoyed her illness.

There was that feeling Caroline had in her bedroom earlier in the day that a powerful force came from the doll. The force seemed stronger than life itself.

She reached for her sweater, thrown over the wicker chair. It was cold at two o'clock in the morning.

As she pulled her sweater on, the envelope that had been stuck in Little Lizzie's box fell out. Caroline had forgotten all about it.

"The History of Little Lizzie," it said. Caroline opened the envelope and found one folded page of brown paper. It felt so old that she thought it might fall apart in her hands.

Carefully, she smoothed it out. Suddenly, she remembered what her father had said. Caroline gasped. Maybe this was it, the strange story he had mentioned.

The writing wasn't English. Caroline thought it was probably French. Nothing was translated.

Why didn't I pay more attention when Dad tried to teach me French? Caroline thought.

There was something else in the envelope. It was a tiny photograph, as old and brown as the paper itself.

The picture was of a woman holding her newborn baby. On the back it read, in curving handwriting, "Annie and her mother, 1890."

Annie and her mother. In 1890?

What had her mom said? The doll has been in the family for over a hundred years!

Think, Caroline told herself. Don't flip out. Think.

Okay, there had been another baby named Annie long ago. No big deal.

Caroline remembered that when they were choosing a name for their baby, her dad had said, "Let's call her Annie if she's a girl. That's an old family name of ours. But it hasn't been used for years."

Mom and Caroline had agreed happily.

Annie was a pretty name.

So who was this other Annie? And how was she connected with the story of Little Lizzie?

Caroline looked closely at the photograph. It was incredible.

This little Annie from 1890 looked exactly like Caroline's baby sister. They looked as if they were twins.

Mom's better now, so Dad will pay attention to me, Caroline thought, tucking the envelope under her pillow. First thing in the morning, I've got to get to the bottom of this.

CHAPTER 5

GET A GRIP ON YOURSELF!

Caroline was woken by the sound of her father's voice. His voice was high and loud, and sounded very nervous. He said, "Yes, yes. In here. Please hurry!"

It was still dark. Caroline looked at her clock. Four a.m.

She got out of bed and ran into her parents' bedroom. Dr. Simons was leaning over Mom, who lay in bed, deathly pale.

It looked as if she was hardly breathing. Her hair was stuck to her forehead with sweat. Her eyes were open, but she didn't seem to be seeing anything around her. Her lips were white.

"I just don't understand," Caroline's dad was saying. "She seemed so much better last night, as though she'd gotten over her illness. She was talking, she had something to eat. Now, a few hours later, she's worse than ever."

"I'm afraid we should get your wife to the hospital right away," Dr. Simons said quietly. "I don't know how much time we have."

"What do you mean?" Dad cried. He reached over and grabbed the doctor's arm.

Dr. Simons shook his head and said, "Let's get her to the hospital, then we can do some tests. We'll figure out what's wrong and how to treat her. Come on, Andrew, get a grip on yourself."

"Dad?" said Caroline in a quiet, frightened voice she barely recognized as her own. "Who'll take care of Annie?"

"Can you do that, honey?" her dad asked. "Just for an hour or so while I go to the hospital with Mom? You know how to make Annie a bottle, don't you?"

Her father looked so upset that Caroline replied, as calmly as she could, "Sure, Dad. Don't worry. I'll take care of it." Actually, she felt like bursting into tears.

Soon the ambulance arrived.

Mom was too weak to walk, so Dr. Simons had her lifted onto a stretcher.

The ambulance workers gently covered her with a blanket. Then they carefully strapped her in.

Caroline watched, afraid, as her mother moaned and rolled her head from side to side. She was confused and didn't know where she was.

Then the ambulance drove away, red lights flashing and siren screaming.

The whole thing was like something on TV, but it was real. What if her mother didn't come back?

Get a grip on yourself, Caroline thought. That's what Dr. Simons had said, and that's what she had to do.

Annie. She had to take care of Annie.

CHAPTER 6

AN EVIL
MASK

The baby was sleeping in her crib by the bedroom window.

Good, thought Caroline, smiling at Annie. At least someone in the family was staying cool.

Then she noticed Little Lizzie.

The doll was sitting in the shadows behind the door.

It seemed like the doll had been secretly watching them.

The smile that Caroline had seen yesterday, which she thought was a trick of the light, was definitely there. The doll's face looked like an evil mask.

The doll looked like it was really enjoying the awful events. It almost looked as though it was daring Caroline to do something about it.

"You're only a doll," Caroline said, taking a step toward it. "Just a doll." But somehow that didn't make her feel brave.

She grabbed Little Lizzie's hands. Its sharp fingers dug into Caroline's skin.

"Ow!" she cried. She almost dropped the doll.

The doll's face was close to her own. Caroline looked into the big, blue eyes. There was cold anger in them.

Caroline tightened her grip.

"All right," she whispered. "I'm going to get rid of you."

She dragged the doll down the hall to the spare room and kicked the door open.

She pushed it roughly into the box, but its legs stuck out, as if it were fighting her.

Caroline turned the doll around and shoved it in, feet first.

Now the arms stuck out, keeping it from fitting into the box. Even when Caroline pressed the doll's arms to its sides, they popped up again when she let go.

Caroline was sweating. She wrapped her arms tightly around Little Lizzie's body and pushed it toward the box.

She could feel the doll pushing back. The little doll seemed as strong as Caroline. It kept pushing back, away from the box.

Caroline gave one last mighty shove.

Little Lizzie fell forward, and Caroline shut the lid. She found some rope and quickly tied it around the box.

"First thing tomorrow," she said, "you're out of here."

Then she locked the spare room's door.

CHAPTER 7

THE OLD STORY

It was almost five in the morning when Caroline made her way downstairs.

It was creepy to be alone in the house. She turned every light on, and then the television. She had the feeling that a cup of hot chocolate and several slices of toast with peanut butter would make her feel a whole lot better.

"Everything's going to be fine," she said to herself, trying to keep her spirits up. "It just has to be."

The phone rang, and Caroline froze. She picked it up, knowing who it would be. She swallowed hard.

"Dad?" she whispered. "Is Mom okay?"

"They're saying it's a mystery, honey," said her father, his voice sad. He paused, and then said, "They ran all the tests, and they can't seem to figure out what's wrong with her. They're saying it might be something new, something they've never seen before. They're just not sure."

"Please come home, Dad." Caroline's voice was shaking. "I'm really scared. It's weird here at night."

"I will," her dad said. "Very soon. The doctor said to ask you, was there anything your mom ate yesterday, or anywhere she went? Is there anything that might be a clue about what's wrong with her?"

"Little Lizzie," Caroline whispered. "Ever since that doll came, Mom's been sick."

"For heaven's sake, Caroline!" her dad cried.

"Dad, I know how crazy it sounds, but you said there was a mystery or a story about Little Lizzie. Can you remember what it was? Please, Dad, it's important!" Caroline said. She was trying not to cry.

"There was some old strange story, but I don't remember it. . . ." Her father's voice trailed off.

"Listen, Dad," Caroline said. "I found a story that was in the box with Little Lizzie. It's in French. If you could translate it, that's where the clue might be."

She waited for him to say something.

Her father was quiet. Then he said, "I have to go. The doctor is here. I'll be home soon. Just be my brave girl."

"But, Dad, the story!" Caroline cried.

Her father hung up.

Caroline put down the phone and leaned against the bookcase.

She had gotten her love of books from her father, who kept hundreds of books stacked in tall shelves in the living room. She felt better just being near them.

She glanced at the closest one.

Grimm's Fairy Tales. Her father had read the stories to her when she was a kid.

Next to that was a thick book with "French-English Dictionary" printed in gold on the spine.

Of course!

She could translate the story herself, or enough of it to make sense.

She dragged the book from the shelf and dumped it next to the phone.

Then she raced upstairs and got the envelope from under her pillow. She also rattled the spare room door. It was still firmly locked.

Back downstairs, Caroline smoothed out the old piece of paper and opened the dictionary.

Where should she begin?

Then she noticed there were some words that appeared more often in the story. Caroline realized that those words must be important

She started looking up those words.

"The baby."

"Helpless."

"Angry."

"The doll."

Finally, she looked up a word that meant death.

"Death. The mother. The baby. Helpless. Angry. The doll."

"The baby."

Annie!

A squeal came from the bedroom. It was Annie.

Caroline thought of Little Lizzie.

It was up there.

Was it after Annie?

CHAPTER 8

AN AXE

Just then, every light in the house turned off at the same time.

Caroline couldn't scream. Her throat was frozen.

She made it to the stairs but tripped halfway up, fell back, and twisted her ankle. Terrified, she kept crawling. Annie's screams became louder and more intense.

Caroline limped to Annie's bedroom door and turned the knob.

It was locked.

She threw her whole weight against the door, but it was no use. It didn't move.

She howled in frustration and beat her fists on the thick wooden panels.

Then she remembered the axe in the spare room.

She went to the spare room and found the axe.

Then she hurried back to Annie's room. She swung the axe at the thick wooden door with all the strength in her body.

The wood began to splinter just above the lock.

After what seemed like forever, there was just enough room for Caroline to squeeze her hand through and unlock the door from the inside.

Suddenly Annie's screams stopped.

Caroline burst into the room. It was very dark, but near the window, a pool of silvery moonlight bathed the crib that her baby sister was in.

Little Lizzie was sitting beside Annie.

The doll's head was leaning forward as if it was staring at the baby.

The moonlight shined on the doll's blond hair and turned it white.

The doll's hands were on Annie's little throat.

Caroline screamed. "If you hurt my sister," she yelled, "I'll . . . I'll . . ."

She ran toward Little Lizzie. But the doll was so strong. It fought back when Caroline pulled it away from Annie.

Caroline looked into the horrible, cold blue eyes and saw the doll's awful smile.

Then she and Little Lizzie hit the floor together, rolling over and over.

The doll wasn't as big as Caroline, but its body was hard and strong, and its sharp fingers dug into Caroline's throat.

Caroline grabbed a handful of Little Lizzie's hair in her fist. She yanked as hard as she could, once, twice, three times.

Little Lizzie pushed harder and harder on Caroline's throat.

Caroline was fighting for her life.

With the strength she had left, she tore the doll's head off and threw it across the room. It crashed against the wall and rolled into the middle of the floor.

Little Lizzie's body lay on its back, with its hands still raised.

Caroline rubbed her neck. She was sobbing in huge gulps.

"Annie!" Caroline cried. She got up, ran to Annie's crib, and lifted the baby up. She held her sister tight.

The baby wasn't breathing.

Caroline hit her hard on the back and Annie coughed. Then she took a big breath and screamed her lungs out.

"Shush," Caroline whispered. "It's all right now. The doll can't hurt us anymore." Then Caroline heard something moving.

She looked up. Her blood turned cold.

Little Lizzie was standing.

Headless, and with its arms stretched out, it began walking toward Caroline with slow, jerky steps.

Caroline screamed.

Just then, her father rushed into the room. He kicked the doll in the chest, hard.

The body hit the wall with a loud crash and lay, with its chest caved in, next to the head.

Then Caroline's father gathered both of his daughters into his arms. "Caroline, Annie, are you all right?" he cried. "I was at the hospital when your mom started talking. We thought she was delirious. She kept saying, 'Don't let Little Lizzie near me! Keep it away!' Suddenly I remembered the old family story about the doll, and it all started to make sense. My mother used to say the story was nothing but a fairy tale. I'm so sorry, Caroline. I didn't believe you. Just tell me you're all right. Please!"

He hugged Caroline tightly.

After Caroline told him that both she and Annie were fine, their father calmed down.

First, he fixed the fuse that had gone out. Then, as the three of them sat close together on the living room couch, Dad told Caroline the story of Little Lizzie.

The story of the doll began long ago, in the year 1890.

A woman named Louise Montand had a baby named Annie.

Louise ordered a very beautiful doll to be made for the baby to play with.

The doll, Little Lizzie, came from a very famous dollmaker in France.

It would be perfect in every way.

The dollmaker was a real artist and worked hard to make something very special.

But the cost was high.

It was too high, according to the family.

The family forced the old man had to sell Little Lizzie to them for not very much money.

He was furious.

He said they would be sorry.

He said that he would curse the doll and the family would pay the greatest price for treating him badly.

No one took the old man seriously, of course, and Little Lizzie was delivered.

Within two days, Louise came down with a fever and Annie was found dead.

The doll was stored away for years, but eventually it was brought out again.

There were no problems then. Nothing bad happened and no one got sick.

Caroline's dad told her, "So Little Lizzie was handed down to different children in the family. As I said, the family ignored the whole story. I remember my mother saying it was a silly old story."

Her dad shook his head.

"Annie! It must be that name, Dad. That's what the old man cursed," Caroline said. She paused when the phone rang.

She stared at her father, afraid.

"Yes, doctor?" Caroline's father asked.

Relief flooded his face and he smiled at Caroline.

"She woke up? Really? She's back to normal. Yes, yes, it's amazing. What did you say? She asked about a doll? Please tell her not to worry. That doll is gone, once and for all. We threw it away. It won't be seen again."

THE HISTORY OF
LITTLE LIZZIE

CHAPTER 9

ANYTHING
FOR ANNIE

"**L**ook, Dad!" A little girl had spotted bright blond hair in a trash can.

"Goodness," said her father, "someone threw away a beautiful doll."

The girl picked up the doll's head and tried to fit it back on the neck. "Can you fix her, Dad? Can you?" she asked excitedly.

The man looked at the doll. It wasn't so badly broken. "Of course I can," he said.

The girl hugged the doll's body and rocked her gently. "Look, it says on her tag that her name is Little Lizzie. Let's take her home. Please."

"Of course, darling!" the man said. "Anything for my little Annie."

About the Author

Janine Burke is the award-winning author of fifteen books of art history, biography, and fiction. She has put together art exhibitions, written for newspapers and journals, and acted as a consultant for films and documentaries.

About the Illustrator

Shaun Tan was born in 1974 and grew up in Australia. Shaun began drawing and painting images for science fiction and horror stories in small-press magazines as a teenager. Since then he has received numerous awards for his picture books. He has recently worked for Blue Sky Studios and Pixar, providing concept artwork for upcoming films.

GLOSSARY

ambulance (AM-byuh-lunhss)—a vehicle that takes sick or injured people to the hospital

axe (AKS)—a tool with a sharp blade on the end of the handle, used for chopping wood

curse (KURSS)—an evil spell that will harm someone

dictionary (DIK-shuh-nare-ee)—a book that lists words and explains what they mean

force (FORSS)—strength or power

fuse (FYOOZ)—a safety device in electrical equipment that cuts off the power if something goes wrong

mystery (MISS-tur-ee)—something that is hard to explain or understand

stretcher (STRECH-ur)—a piece of canvas attached to two poles, used for carrying a sick or injured person

translate (TRANZ-late)—to change words from one language into another

DISCUSSION QUESTIONS

1. Can you think of some stories in your life or that you've read in books or seen in movies that are like the story of Little Lizzie? Do you believe in strange old stories like that one?

2. Have you ever been left in charge of a baby or little kid, like Caroline was with Annie in this book? How did you handle it? Were you nervous?

3. Caroline's mother becomes very sick in this book. What are some ways to help a sick person? What would you do if someone you loved were very sick?

WRITING PROMPTS

1. At the end of this book, a little girl finds Little Lizzie in a trash can. Write another chapter of this book and tell what happens to the little girl and her family when Little Lizzie is taken to their house.

2. In this book, Caroline used to collect dolls. Do you collect anything? Some kids collect old coins, stamps, action figures, or comic books. Make a list of the things in your collection. Why do you collect those things? Why are they special to you?

3. Sometimes it can be cool to see events from another point of view. Try writing Chapter 8 from Little Lizzie's point of view. How would the doll think and talk about the things that happen in that chapter?

TAKE A DEEP BREATH AND

TRAPPED

BY JAMES MOLONEY

STONE ARCH *Fantasy*

David's new town is boring until he discovers a big drainpipe that looks perfect for skateboarding. He can't resist exploring the huge cement tunnel. Then he hears something odd. Someone else is inside the tunnel, in the darkness, where no living person should be.

STEP INTO THE SHADE!

Gavin is obsessed with hunting for treasure with his metal detector. He finds the perfect spot — a huge, sandy playground. Then he meets a bunch of kids who have a mysterious treasure hunt of their own. Gavin gets the feeling they want him to stay . . . forever.

INTERNET SITES

Do you want to know more about subjects related to this book? Or are you interested in learning about other topics? Then check out FactHound, a fun, easy way to find Internet sites.

Our investigative staff has already sniffed out great sites for you!

Here's how to use FactHound:

1. Visit *www.facthound.com*

2. Select your grade level.

3. To learn more about subjects related to this book, type in the book's ISBN number: **1598898582**.

4. Click the **Fetch It** button.

FactHound will fetch the best Internet sites for you!

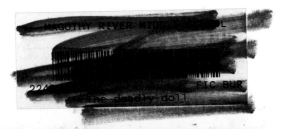